Get Set for a Pet Hen

By Gianni Giambiccolo

Illustrated by Jerry Tiritilli

C0-ARB-672

Target Skill Short *Ee*/e/

PEARSON
Scott Foresman

Get set, Meg. Go!

Meg met Ted here.

Meg can get Hen.

Hen is a pet for Meg!

Hen, get in the pen.

Look! Meg fed Hen.

Get in bed, Hen!